A NOTE FROM THE AUTHOR

When I was small, the kitchen was the place I felt the most coddled, cozy, and happy. Baking with Mom was one of my favorite things. I had her all to myself, and we would chat about school and sing silly songs.

I would lick the bowl and she would wipe my face. Teamwork!

Jess Mikhail draws the pictures

Eva Katzler writes the stories

I grew up with two busy working parents, but I never noticed an absence. Quality time spent together as a family was their top priority and filled me with a sense of safety and calm that still remains with me. Whether I was cleaning the candlesticks with Mom (polishing pirates' treasure) or helping Dad tidy up the yard (chatting to pixies in the forest), I was playing, enjoying being with my parents, and having the time of my life.

Florentine and Pig is a safe, imaginative, and fun-filled world that encourages families to read, play, and create together. It celebrates the imagination of little ones and champions parents' loving and creative relationships with their children.

I cherish my childhood memories, and I hope that *Florentine and Pig* will inspire parents to fill their own children's memory banks with silly times, messy times, and most important, good-fun family times.

I can't wait to hear all about them . . .

All the recipes and crafts in this book have been designed for children to make with help from a responsible adult, so grab your aprons and tape and jump on board!

Eva X

Laura and Jess Tilli make up the recipes and arty bits

For more recipes, crafts, and ideas, please pop over to **www.florentineandpig.com** or become our fan on Facebook— we'd love to see you there!

Remember, sharp knives and hot things can be dangerous.
Adults should supervise children closely when cooking and crafting.

To Mum, Dad, and Benchick.
Bestest team everest —E. K.

To Kathleen, who also likes to
dance while cooking —J. M.

Text copyright © 2012 by Eva Katzler
Illustrations copyright © 2012 by Jess Mikhail
Recipes devised and crafts co-devised by Laura and Jess Tilli
Wallpaper reproduced by kind permission of Elanbach
All rights reserved. No part of this book may be reproduced or transmitted in any form
or by any means, electronic or mechanical, including photocopying, recording, or by any
information storage and retrieval system, without permission in writing from the publisher.

First published in Great Britain in June 2012 by Bloomsbury Publishing Plc
Published in the United States of America in June 2012
by Bloomsbury Books for Young Readers
www.bloomsburykids.com

For information about permission to reproduce selections from this book, write to
Permissions, Bloomsbury BFYR, 175 Fifth Avenue, New York, New York 10010

Library of Congress Cataloging-in-Publication Data
Katzler, Eva.
Florentine and Pig / by Eva Katzler ; illustrations by Jess Mikhail. — 1st U.S. ed.
p.   cm.
Summary: After a week of rain, Florentine and Pig are ready to do something outdoors and decide to have a picnic,
but getting the apples needed for Pig's favorite treat proves to be a challenge. Includes directions for making
"Pig's Pretty Picnic Bunting" and recipes for "Apple and carrot muffins with sunshine lemon icing" and
"Florentine's homemade pink lemonade with fresh berry ice cubes."
ISBN 978-1-59990-847-2 (hardcover) • ISBN 978-1-59990-989-3 (reinforced)
[1. Picnics—Fiction. 2. Cooking—Fiction. 3. Pigs—Fiction.] I. Title.
PZ7.K1579Flo 2012   [E]—dc23   2011042336

Typeset in Bembo, Boopee, and Eeyore
Book design by Bloomsbury Children's Design

Printed in China by C&C Offset Printing Co., Ltd., Shenzhen, Guangdong
2 4 6 8 10 9 7 5 3 1 (hardcover)
2 4 6 8 10 9 7 5 3 1 (reinforced)

All papers used by Bloomsbury Publishing, Inc., are natural, recyclable products
made from wood grown in well-managed forests. The manufacturing processes
conform to the environmental regulations of the country of origin.

Florentine and Pig

Eva Katzler

illustrated by Jess Mikhail

recipes and crafts by Laura and Jess Tilli

BLOOMSBURY

NEW YORK BERLIN LONDON SYDNEY

Florentine and Pig were having breakfast one sparkly morning. "Now that the sun is warm and toasty, I think we should do something outside," said Florentine.

"Oh, Pig, I have a wonderful idea! We should have a picnic!"

Pig liked the sound of a picnic very much.

"We need to think of our favorite things to eat," Florentine said.
"I love honey and YOU love crunchy apples."

Florentine began scribbling
in her notebook.

The pencil was moving so
speedy fast it made Pig's
eyes go big and funny.

florentine and Pig's very lovely picnic

Apple + carrot muffins with sunshine lemon icing

Rainbow sprinkle cookies

Cheddar cheese + pumpkin seed bites

Sticky red onion hummus with cucumber dunkers

Green pea picnic-time tarts

Florentine's homemade pink lemonade with fresh berry ice cubes

At last, Florentine revealed all the marvelous things they would make.

Pig's eyes got bigger and blinkier.

He thought Florentine was very clever to think up such a wonderful picnic.

"Oh no, Pig!"
Florentine gasped.
"You ate our very last
apple for breakfast!"

"How will we make our muffins now?"

Just as Florentine had said, Pig could
not see any more apples on their
apple tree.

"Oh dear," said Florentine.
"What are we going to do? Pig?"

"Pig?"

"Pig, where are you?"

Florentine couldn't see Pig anywhere!

Just then, Pig burst back into the kitchen with such a crash that all the pots and pans wobbled and rang and clattered and banged!

He was carrying his shiny telescope!

He pointed it at their apple tree, shut one eye,
and peered through the telescope with the other.

(Pig was very good at winking.)

Suddenly, Pig began jumping in the air excitedly!
"What is it, Pig?" Florentine asked. "What can you see?"

Right at the very tippy-top of their apple tree were three of the **biggest**, **reddest**, **juiciest**, and **crunchiest** apples she had ever seen.

"Well I never!" exclaimed Florentine.

"Those apples look quite tricky to reach, Pig," said Florentine. "How will we get them down?"

But Pig was already marching around the kitchen collecting everything he needed for his crunchy apple mission.

Pig loved apples very much, and nothing—but nothing—was going to stop him from having them for his picnic.

Nothing at all.

Florentine and Pig set off into the yard with everything they needed (plus a strawberry jam sandwich, in case Pig got hungry).

Armed with his wooden spoon, Pig waved good-bye to Florentine and disappeared up the ladder.

"You're so brave, Pig," called Florentine from under the tree. "Be careful, please!"

Florentine watched and listened . . .

She heard **rustling**
and **bustling** as Pig
bravely bashed the
big leaves out of
his way with his
wooden spoon.

She heard **bumping**
and **thumping** as the tree
branches **banged** against
the bowl on Pig's head.

She heard **chomping** and **chewing**
as Pig munched on his strawberry jam sandwich.

And then all was quiet.

Florentine waited . . .

and waited . . .

and waited.

But she couldn't hear **anything at all.**

"ARE YOU OKAY, PIG?"
Florentine shouted.
"ARE YOU STUCK?"

After a moment there was a loud
rustling and a wild swishing of
the leaves at the top of the tree.
Suddenly Florentine heard
three very loud snaps.

SNAP!

SNAP!

SNAP!

Then there was

a great thrashing

and a thwacking

and a crashing

and a whooshing!

When Florentine looked up,
she glimpsed a flash of red-and-
white spottiness tumbling toward
the ground!

When all the noise had stopped,
Florentine peeked through her fingers.

She could see the rope swinging gently
at the bottom of the tree, and hanging
at the end of it was . . .

a very happy upside-down Pig.

Bundled up inside
Pig's tablecloth were
three very **red**,
very **juicy**,
very **crunchy**
apples!

"Oh, Pig, you're the best," said Florentine. "Now we have everything we need! Let's get cooking."

They rolled up their sleeves, they washed their hands, and then they were ready to begin!

Florentine baked
and caked
and mixed
and whipped,

Pig slurped
and sloshed
and laughed
and licked!

Florentine chopped
and chunked
and danced
and diced,

Sugar

Pig whisked
and wiggled
and stirred
and sliced!

Florentine dipped
and dunked
and cooked
and crunched,

and they tossed
and twirled
and mashed
and munched!

When everything was
ready, they laid their
blanket beneath the apple
tree and brought out all
the delicious food.

Florentine sighed happily. "What a
wonderful picnic," she said. "I have
loved every single minute!"

But Pig was already fast asleep and
snoring very loudly.

Florentine giggled.

It was then that she noticed
Pig had something . . .

. . . right on the end of his nose.

The End ... Ta da!

Apple and Carrot Muffins with Sunshine Lemon Icing

Makes 6

For the muffins

⅓ c brown sugar

⅓ c soft butter

1 free-range egg

1 tbsp plain yogurt

½ c self-rising flour

1 tsp baking powder

1 apple (cored and grated)

1 carrot (peeled and grated)

1 tsp cinnamon

For the icing

⅓ c cream cheese

1½ c confectioner's sugar

Juice of half a lemon

1 Preheat your oven to 350°F.

2 Beat the sugar and butter together in a big bowl with a wooden spoon until it's nice and creamy.

3 Add the egg and yogurt and mix again.

4 Mix in the flour, baking powder, apple, carrot, and cinnamon.

5 Line a muffin pan with 6 paper baking cups and plop a big teaspoonful of your mixture into each cup.

6 Pop in the oven for 25 minutes or until lightly golden. (When you poke a toothpick into the middle of a muffin and it comes out clean, you know they're done!)

7 While the muffins cool on a wire rack, mix all your icing ingredients together until smooth and creamy.

8 Dollop the icing on top of your delicious muffins and enjoy! Yum!

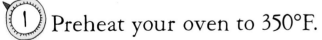

The muffins may sink a bit when they come out of the oven, but don't worry!

Rainbow Sprinkle Cookies

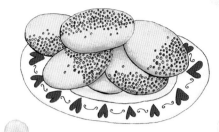

For the cookies

1 c soft butter
½ c sugar
1¼ c plain flour

For the rainbows

3 tbsp confectioner's sugar
Juice of half a lemon
1 jar of colored sprinkles

1. Preheat your oven to 350°F.

2. Put the butter and sugar into a big bowl and beat with a wooden spoon until soft and creamy.

3. Add the flour, mixing with a spoon first, then when it gets doughy put your hands in the bowl and bring it together into a big ball.

4. Divide the mixture into 12 pieces the size of ping-pong balls and place on a baking sheet, flattening them a bit with your hands.

5. Pop in the oven for 15 minutes or until lightly golden, then cool on a wire rack.

6. To make your rainbows, mix the confectioner's sugar and lemon juice until smooth. Pour out the sprinkles into a separate bowl.

7. Dip half of each cooled cookie into the icing and then into the sprinkles, then place them on a tray to set. Delicious!

Cheddar Cheese and Pumpkin Seed Bites

Makes 6

You will need

½ c rolled oats
½ c grated cheddar cheese
2½ tbsp soft butter
1 small handful toasted pumpkin seeds
2 tsp chopped fresh rosemary
   (or 1 tsp dried)
1 free-range egg, beaten

1 Preheat your oven to 350°F.

2 In a big bowl, mix all the ingredients together really well until you've got a big cheesy, seedy mixture.

3 Line a muffin pan with 6 paper cups and divide the mixture between them.

4 Pop in the oven for 30 minutes or until golden brown.

5 Leave to cool (don't worry if the egg has made little bubbles on them—they will soon disappear!), then gobble them up with your best friends.

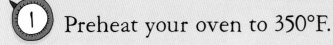

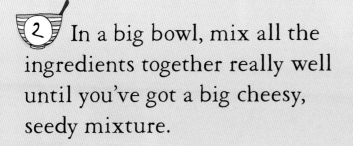

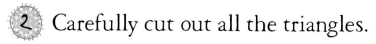

Pig's Pretty Picnic Bunting

You will need

A 6" x 6" x 4" cardboard triangle as a template

Scraps of pretty paper and cardboard—
  wallpaper, wrapping paper, napkins,
  doilies, whatever you can find!

Scissors

Glue

String

1 Use your template to draw triangles on all your scraps of paper.

2 Carefully cut out all the triangles.

3 If the paper is plain on one side, you can stick two triangles together back-to-back with glue.

4 Lay out a long piece of string and arrange your triangles along it, a few inches apart.

5 Make sure the string is on top of the straight edge of each triangle, not across the point.

6 Fold over the edge of each triangle to hide the string, and stick it down with glue.

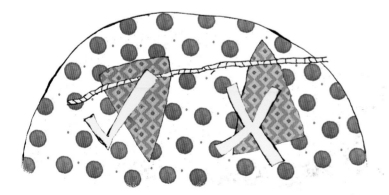

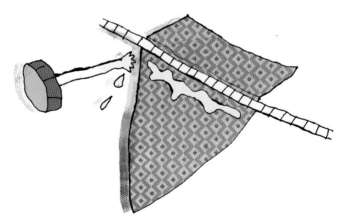

You're done! Now hang your pretty bunting up in the yard or wherever you're having your picnic!

For 6 friends

Sticky Red Onion Hummus with Cucumber Dunkers

For the sticky onions
1 red onion
2 tsp sugar
5 tbsp balsamic vinegar
2½ tbsp water

For the hummus
1 8-oz can of chickpeas, drained
4 tbsp olive oil
Juice of half a lemon
Pinch of salt and pepper
1 clove of garlic, peeled and
   squashed with the back of a spoon

For the dunkers
Half a cucumber, cut into spears
   for dunking.

1. Have a grown-up carefully slice your onion as thin as possible and put it in a nonstick pan with the sugar, vinegar, and water.

2. Cook on very low heat for 20 minutes or until the onions have become a golden, sticky goo. Be very careful not to touch the mixture at this stage—it's piping hot! Turn the heat off and leave to cool.

3. Put all the ingredients for the hummus into a big bowl and mix with a hand blender (or mash well with a potato masher).

4. Spoon your hummus into a bowl and pile your sticky onions on top.

5. Arrange your cucumber dunkers on a plate and dunk away!

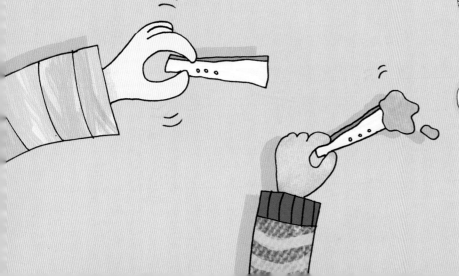

Green pea picnic-time Tarts

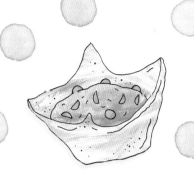

Makes 6

You will need

6 slices of whole wheat bread, crusts cut off (just this once!)

Olive oil spray

1 free-range egg, beaten

3 tbsp sour cream

A big handful of freshly grated parmesan cheese

3 tbsp frozen peas, thawed

1 green onion, snipped into small pieces with scissors (make sure you use the green parts too!)

1 Preheat your oven to 350°F.

2 Using your hands, flatten each piece of bread slightly and spray both sides with the olive oil.

3 Line each cup of a muffin pan with one slice of bread and pop in the oven for 10 minutes until the bread is just starting to turn golden.

4 In a bowl, mix together the egg, the sour cream, and most of the grated cheese.

5 Divide the peas and the green onion evenly between the bread cups. Then slowly pour a little of the egg mixture into each one. Be careful not to overfill the cups!

6 Sprinkle the last bit of the grated cheese over each tart and pop in the oven for 15 minutes or until they are set and golden . . . Mmm!

Florentine's Homemade Pink Lemonade with Fresh Berry Ice Cubes

For 6 friends

For the ice cubes

A big handful of fresh berries—
strawberries, raspberries, or blueberries

For the lemonade

A big bottle of seltzer water
5 lemons
2 tbsp pomegranate juice
6 tbsp honey

1 Pop one or two berries into
each compartment of an ice cube
tray. Fill with water and freeze
overnight.

2 Pour the seltzer water into a big
pitcher and squeeze in the juice of
4 lemons.

3 Ask an adult to cut the last
lemon into chunks (with the peel
still on!) and add to the seltzer.

4 Pour the pomegranate juice
into the seltzer.

5 Stir in the honey and add your
beautiful berry ice cubes just before
you serve it to your thirsty friends.